Karin Lorentzen

Lanky Longlegs

illustrated by Jan Ormerod

translated from the Norwegian by Joan Tate

A Margaret K. McElderry Book
Atheneum   1983   New York

Library of Congress catalog number: 82-72246
ISBN 0-689-50260-5
© 1976 by Gyldendal Norsk Forlag A/S
English translation © 1982 by Joan Tate
Illustrations © 1982 by Jan Ormerod
Printed in Great Britain
First American Edition

Contents

Lanky Longlegs

"Lanky Longlegs," Di whispered to herself. She was lying on her back in the grass, looking up at the empty, blue sky.

"Lanky Longlegs," she whispered slightly louder, trying to get used to the name.

"*Lanky Longlegs*," she shouted up into the air, and the words echoed back at her.

Her real name was Diana Christine Sophie Mathilda Cooper. That's what she had been known as until yesterday, and then she had been given a new name at school. A boy called Martin Landale had invented it.

"You're as lanky as your name is long," he'd said.

Di had never thought her name especially long before. She had been called after both her grandmothers, Diana Christine, and Sophie Mathilda, and she was proud of her names.

At school, they had all been asked to stand up and introduce themselves to Martin, who was a new boy, and when Diana had produced all her grandmothers' names, he had started laughing.

"Di Lanky-Longlegs," he had said. "That suits you much better."

Diana Christine. No, that was wrong. That was yesterday. Di was today. She raised her legs in

1

the air and kicked them about.

Lanky Longlegs. It wasn't a nice name, in fact it was rather nasty. It sounded like "Daddy Long-legs", and no one liked them. She rolled up the trouser-legs of her jeans and looked at her legs. They were long and thin, her thighs, too.

She had been the tallest in the class until yesterday. Today she was second tallest, because Martin was even taller. He was broader, too, so he didn't seem so tall.

Di let her legs fall back to the ground, pulled up a piece of grass, put it between her thumbs and blew through it. A sharp note screeched through the air, like a whistle, but different.

Small, white clouds were drifting across the sky, changing as the sun shone on them, some-times blindingly white and dark at the same time. They slid into each other and turned into people, trolls and fairytale people. But then the autumn wind came along and blew the fairytale away, the clouds moved on and the people vanished. She blew on the grass stem again, feeling her lips tickling.

Di was nine, with short, curly hair and long legs. She was very like her father. He was an architect and worked in an office, designing houses. Not high-rise apartment houses, but long, low houses in terraces with small gardens. Di was lying in a

garden just like that at this moment, waiting for her mother and Michael to come home.

Her mother worked at Mr Wild's, the travel agent, just near her school, and Mike was looked after by Sister Anna, who lived across the road.

Sister Anna was a nurse at the hospital for three nights a week, so she was able to look after Mike in the mornings, when Mum was at work. Mike was Di's little brother, two years old and very like her.

Di was used to waiting for them and didn't mind being on her own. She was used to that, too. She lay there feeling pleased. She liked feeling pleased, and sometimes the pleasure of feeling pleased was greater than the actual thing she was pleased about.

Like yesterday, for instance. Di had been feeling sorry for herself when she got back from school, fed up with the new boy and her new name. Everything was stupid and the only good thing was that Mum and Mike were coming. Di had felt pleased at the thought. But then Mike had been bad-tempered and Mum tired.

When Di told her mother about the new boy and her new name, Mum had started to laugh.

"Lanky Longlegs," she said. "I was called that too, when I was your age."

She had been about to say something else, but then Mike had started screaming and instead her mother had asked Di to go to the shop and buy

4

some groceries. She hadn't said anything about the new name until much later that evening. When Mike had gone to bed and she and Dad and Di were together in the living room, she started talking about it again.

"You know what, Harold," she said, "Di's being called Lanky Longlegs by the boys in her class. Does that remind you of anything?"

"Yes." He looked at Mum over the top of his glasses and smiled slyly.

Suddenly Mum leaped up and pulled up her skirt, showing her long, thin legs.

"Guess who called me Lanky Longlegs, Di?"

Di shook her head, looking at her mother's slim legs. "I don't know."

"A boy with fair, curly hair and blue eyes. He was two years older than I was and the most horrible boy in the world. His name was Harold."

Mum leaned over Dad and put her arms around his neck.

"But you called me Goggle Eyes," said Dad, laughing so much that the newspaper crackled.

Di looked at them. She liked it when they played the fool. It made her feel warm inside and out. Mum rocked from side to side and Dad rocked with her.

Dad and Mum. Goggle Eyes and Lanky Longlegs.

It was awful, really, but nice in a way, too.

"Then the years went by and Goggle Eyes

and Lanky Longlegs grew up and one day they decided to get married."

They went on rocking.

"Lanky Longlegs decided," said Dad. He sounded quite serious.

"But Goggle Eyes popped the question."

Dad laughed and stretched out his hand to Di. She crept into his lap, happy to feel his arms around her.

Di smiled to herself, thinking about Mum and Dad. Then she thought about Martin. He didn't wear glasses, thank goodness.

The wind grew stronger and a large black cloud drifted in front of the sun.

Di pulled down the legs of her jeans. She gathered up her school books, pushed them into her satchel and let herself into the house.

Michael

Fendy, a large, black Rottweiler, stayed in her basket in the hall when Di came in, lifting her head and pricking up her ears as if listening.

Di flung down her satchel and ran across to the dog. She got down on the floor and stroked Fendy's head.

"How're your puppies, then?" Di put her hand carefully on the large, round stomach. "Are they coming soon?" she went on, rubbing the taut skin between Fendy's nipples.

"Come on, Fendy, out with you. Fresh air first, then you'll have your milk."

Di grasped the dog's collar with both hands and pulled. Reluctantly, Fendy allowed herself to be dragged out of her basket. She got up sluggishly, her stomach swaying from side to side as she walked.

Di opened the door and Fendy lumbered down the two steps outside.

Afterwards, she was given her milk. Then she climbed back into her basket.

Yesterday, Fendy had taken Di's bedspread and made a bundle out of it, and now the bundle was in her basket. She wanted to have it for her puppies.

Di lay down beside Fendy's basket resting her

head gently on Fendy's back and taking one of her ears in her hand. It was nice to feel.

Di rubbed the tip of the ear between her fingers, and Fendy lay still. She was used to it. Ever since she was small, Di had lain like that, curled around and holding her ear. She would rub it between her fingers, using it like a comforter, while sucking her other thumb.

Di had long since stopped sucking her thumb, but she still rubbed Fendy's ear.

Di cautiously felt Fendy's bulging stomach, noting the hard, little lumps that she could move.

Fendy lay there quite calmly, knowing Di was feeling her puppies and letting her do so.

They were to be Fendy's first puppies, but although she had never had lumps in her stomach before, she knew what kind of lumps they were.

Last night Fendy had taken Di's ragdoll to bed with her. She had licked it and carried it in her mouth like a bone. Afterwards, she had hidden it behind the sofa in the living room with the bedspread.

Di had found them both there, and she had washed the doll while Mum had done the bedspread. But early this morning, Fendy had again dragged the bedspread into her basket. It was still there.

"'Lo, Di!" The door flew open with a bang, and Mike ran in.

Mum came in behind him, carrying a plastic

bag full of shopping. Good. Di wouldn't have to do it.

She felt a quick flash of pleasure.

Mike at once got on top of her.

Di pushed him away.

"You mustn't. Think of her puppies! Supposing you squashed them to death?"

Mike didn't understand anything about puppies or squashing them to death.

They went out into the kitchen. Mum had tipped all the groceries on to the table and Di helped her put them away.

"How was school today?" asked Mum, handing her the milk carton.

"Not bad. Martin still calls me Lanky Longlegs. I wish he'd stop, and call me Di, instead."

Di put the milk carton into the refrigerator.

"Can I have some bread and cream cheese?" She got out the loaf and started cutting it.

"Give Mike some, too, and then put him to bed for me afterwards, will you?"

Mike loved cream cheese. He licked the slice of bread and dug his tongue into it to get as much as possible. It was a mess and the bread fell to pieces.

"Pig! What a way to eat! Look at your face. You've got cream cheese up to your ears."

Di pointed at his ears.

"'Lo, Di," said Mike, laughing and licking around his mouth.

"You're hopeless, poppet." Di took his head in her hands and pressed it to her. Then she lifted him out of his chair and carried him into the bedroom. As quickly as she could she washed and changed him.

Mike put his thumb in his mouth as soon as he was under the quilt, licking off the rest of the cream cheese before starting to suck. At the same time, he put his forefinger on his nose and rubbed it up and down.

Di stood looking at him, remembering that time long ago when Mike had been inside Mum, and Dad was in bed with 'flu.

Dad had coughed and sneezed germs all over the house and Di had caught them. The germs had settled in her nose and blocked it up, and then she had had a headache and high temperature.

Mum had held her stomach and asked Mike not to come until all the germs were out of the house.

But Michael had come, all the same.

Just when everything was at its very worst.

Sister Anna had gone with Mum to the hospital and Dad had coughed into a mound of paper handkerchiefs.

Di was hardly allowed to see Mike when Mum came home with him. Mum had stood in the crack of the door and shown her a little, red face, buried in a mass of woolly blankets.

Di had wanted to hold Mike, take his tiny

fingers in hers and touch his fine hair.

But she wasn't allowed to.

She wasn't allowed to sit on Mum's lap either, and she had wanted to so much. She wanted to cuddle right up close to Mum and feel her heart beating.

She hadn't felt it for months and months, for that big stomach had been in the way, shutting out her heart.

Mum had comforted her through the door and said she was afraid of infection and that Michael would be ill, too. So Di had to understand and be a big girl.

Mum had looked tired, her face thin, with dark shadows under her eyes. Di had cried.

She didn't want to be a big girl. She didn't want to understand anything. She just wanted Mum to herself, all to herself. Without Mike. He could go back to the hospital, then Mum needn't be afraid of him catching anything.

Mum had stood in the door and cried too, and said she was just as miserable as Di was, and the only thing she wanted to do in the whole world was to hug away all their misery. But she dared not. Michael might catch those horrid germs.

Michael never caught those horrid germs and every single one of them had gone away in the end.

Mum became her old self again, just as before, her eyes bright, and Di was allowed to feel her heart beating.

Di stroked Mike's hair, feeling the damp curls tickling her fingers.

Then she sat down carefully on the edge of the bed and took one of his hands in hers. It was small and warm and at once clasped her finger.

Di stayed there looking at his little head and red cheeks. She simply couldn't take it in—not when he was lying there like that, looking so healthy. Not when he pulled his finger out of his mouth with a plop and smiled broadly. Not when he had such fine red cheeks.

She couldn't understand it.

But she had seen him different, too, pale and quiet. Ill.

But that was long ago. That was in the spring, and Mum and Dad had been awfully serious, sad and serious, and Mike had had to go to the hospital.

While he was there, Dad had told Di about his illness, and what was wrong with him.

Dad had looked old when he had told her. Di remembered sitting on the very edge of the chair and staring down at her shoes. She hadn't said a word. She had wanted to, but the words simply wouldn't come. They seemed to have been trapped inside her, whirling around and around without coming out.

"Is Mike going to die?" The words had slipped out by themselves.

Dad waited for a moment before answering. "We all die in the end, you know. That's life. We are born and we die. But mostly we die when we're old.''

Dad had taken her hand and held on to it hard, and Di had felt his fingers wet with tears.

''Perhaps Mike will never be old.''

Then she understood. Dad didn't have to say anything more.

Di remembered lying awake that night. She had thought everyone who went to the hospital came back well: at least little children.

Mike gradually fell asleep and Di pulled the quilt up over him. Then she closed the door behind her and went out into the kitchen.

''Mum, Helen asked if I could go to the mountains with them next weekend. Can I?''

''Of course you can.''

Mum smiled and put the bread away.

Fendy

Two days later, Fendy began to get restless. She didn't want anything, but just kept walking backwards and forwards across the living room floor, whining.

Dad put some newspapers in her basket, but Fendy walked around them, looking reproachfully at him. Gradually she retreated behind the sofa and started scratching at the carpet. She lay down, scratched, got up, walked around in a circle and then lay down again.

"Isn't there anything we can do for her?" said Di, watching uneasily. Fendy had never behaved like this before and Di didn't like it. She felt tears coming into her eyes.

"No, Fendy'll manage on her own," said Dad, looking at Di. "All we can do is to leave her in peace but let her feel we are with her. Just wait until the pups come, then you'll see how clever she is at managing everything on her own."

Dad disappeared behind his paper again.

Mum was putting Mike to bed and Di could hear laughter coming from his room. She was tickling him, Di could tell that from the way he was laughing. Fendy went on scratching.

"Supposing she spoils the carpet?" said Di, looking at Dad.

"She couldn't do that. But if she does, we can fix it." Dad put his paper down. "Do you know why she goes around in a circle scratching the carpet?" He took off his glasses. "Because when dogs lived in the wild they used to trample down the grass where they wanted to lie. That's why Fendy's always going around and around in her basket, scratching and scraping before she goes to sleep." Dad pulled the sofa away from the wall. "Now she knows the puppies are coming, she wants to make a bed where she can have them."

"But she's got her basket?"

"She doesn't want to get into it. The newspapers frighten her. But when she's had the first pup, we'll take it over to the basket and—you'll see—she'll follow. We'll put your bedspread under her head, so she doesn't notice the newspapers."

"Why have you put the papers in her basket?"

"To save the cushion. When the pups come, they're each in a bag of water, and when Fendy bites a hole in the bag, the water'll run out. That's why."

Dad got up. "Do you want a cup of tea, Di?"

"Yes, please. With lots of milk in it."

Di went to fetch her knitting. She was making a red and white striped scarf for Mike. She put the ball of wool on the sofa and started knitting, the needles clicking against each other.

Fendy was panting noisily behind the sofa,

16

as if she were utterly exhausted.

Di put down her knitting and knelt on the floor behind the sofa. Fendy turned her head when she saw Di leaning over her. Her great stomach was heaving up and down as she panted.

"Fendy, my darling Fendy, beautiful Fendy," crooned Di, stroking her head.

Suddenly a spasm went through the great body. Fendy lifted her head as if she wanted to get up, but she couldn't manage it and her head fell back on to the bedspread.

Then there was another spasm, and Fendy panted hard.

Di didn't know what to do, so she just went on stroking the dark head, comforting her: "Fendy, good girl, Fendy."

Then there was another spasm and Di saw a lump sliding out of Fendy. The lump lay between her back legs. Di was unable to make a sound. She couldn't even call Dad.

"Fendy'll manage it all on her own," he had said.

Fendy started getting up, raising her heavy body halfway and stretching out towards her pup. But then her forelegs gave way, and she fell back without touching it.

Di felt her heart thumping and the words "manage it all on her own" whirled around in her head. But Fendy wasn't managing. She was just lying there.

Di picked up the newborn pup, still in its bag of water, lifting it carefully and putting it between its mother's forelegs.

Fendy sniffed at the pup, pushing it with her nose, then sniffed again. Then she started biting the membrane round the little body, puncturing it so that the water ran out, just as Dad had said, and a wet head came out of the hole.

At once a sharp whimper cut through the air. Then another.

Di felt warm inside. Tears ran down her cheeks and chin, down on to Fendy's coat.

Fendy bit the cord connected to the puppy's belly and went on licking the membrane around the puppy until it had all gone. In the end there was nothing to show for it except a wet patch on the carpet.

"Dad, Dad, Fendy's had her first puppy!"

Di thought she had whispered, but she couldn't have done, because Dad came running.

"Fetch some milk, and tell Mum."

Dad pulled the sofa out further and bent down over Fendy. Then Di came back with the milk.

Fendy drank it all down.

The puppy found a nipple and scrabbled with its tiny paws as its head pushed rhythmically against Fendy.

"I think we'll move them, before the next one comes." Dad shook the little pup to make it let go, but Fendy raised her head and growled.

"Fendy doesn't like you doing that," said Di, taking Dad's hand away.

"You do it then, Di. Maybe Fendy would prefer you to do it."

Di put her hand over the newborn pup and pulled it away from its mother.

"I'm just going to put it in your basket in the hall, and you must come, too," said Di quietly. "Come on, then."

She lifted the puppy up. "Come on, then."

Dad helped Fendy up, and she staggered slightly, as if about to fall, but when she saw Di walking towards the basket, she followed slowly after her.

Dad moved the bedspread to one end of the basket and Di put the pup down in the other. Fendy stood there, reluctant to climb into the basket. It was the newspapers. They looked so hard and cold and Fendy stared at Dad with doleful eyes. Gradually, but reluctantly, she got into the basket.

Di placed the pup close to a nipple, and patted Fendy on the head.

Their tea was cold, so Dad made another pot, and Fendy was given some more milk.

Di took her cup of tea and sat down beside the basket. The pup was shoving with its head and sucking away. Fendy lay with her eyes closed, as if asleep.

19

Then she began panting again and after a spasm had gone through her body, another pup slid out of her. This time Fendy got up, bit a hole in the membrane and started licking. Another little whimper and Fendy had become mother to two puppies.

The third came just after that.

"Dad, how do we know which came first? They look the same."

Di looked at the three, black bodies.

Dad lifted up one of the pups.

"This is the little miss who came first. The rest so far are males."

He put it down again.

"If she has more than one female pup, you can put a piece of wool loosely around the neck of this one."

"I'd love to have that one for my own."

Di stroked the soft fur with her finger. "I was the only one there when it was born."

"I don't know whether we can keep two dogs as big as Fendy," said Dad. "The pups will grow big, you know. But we can talk about that later."

The fourth pup didn't come until an hour later. Mum had gone to bed, Fendy was asleep and the puppies were feeding.

Di grew tired just sitting and looking at them.

"Dad, can't you come and sit here? Then we could watch together," she called, and Dad came, pushing the big brown chair out into the hall. She climbed on to his lap, and he hugged her close.

"Aren't they sweet? Two females and two males, now." Di looked at the thread of red wool hanging around the neck of the first-born. Her puppy. If only she were allowed to keep it!

"Are there many more, do you think?" said Di, trying to hide a yawn.

At that moment, Fendy woke up and Di realized the fifth puppy was on its way.

Di looked at Dad.

"Does it hurt Fendy when the puppies come?"

"I think it's hard rather than painful work for her. She has to press them out, and that's hard work."

Dad pretended to press hard, going red in the face.

"It sounds as if it hurts. When she pants, it's almost as if she's groaning."

Di pressed and groaned.

"The first pup is always the most difficult," Dad said, putting his arm around Di and squeezing her.

Di rubbed her eyes, which were prickling. She tried rubbing away the prickles, but it was no use.

"I think I'll have a little rest," she yawned, snuggling up to Dad.

The Puppies

Di woke with a jerk and sat up in bed. She was trying to remember something; and then she remembered.

The puppies!

She was out of bed in a flash and, forgetting her slippers, ran to the puppies.

Fendy was lying in the basket when she got there. She raised her head and pricked up her ears, just as she usually did, and Di knelt down beside her.

Fendy made a sound of contentment from somewhere deep down in her throat.

A heap of puppies was lying close to her stomach, all of them fast asleep.

How many were there?

Di could only remember five. There must be many more, at least double that number.

She moved some of the puppies to one side and they whimpered and struggled with their legs. Their stomachs were round like balls, their legs thin as sticks, and their heads large and clumsy. Their puppies' ears lay flat on their heads, and their eyes were closed.

They were lovely.

Not really beautiful, but very sweet.

Fendy grew uneasy and Di put the pups down

again, then started counting—four, five, six, seven, *eight* puppies. "Clever girl," said Di, rubbing her cheek against Fendy's forehead, and looking at her.

Suddenly Fendy thrust her nose in amongst

the puppies and pulled out a noisy one that had been lying there whining. She turned him over on his back and licked him. The pup rolled about like a rubber ball and stopped whining.

Then Fendy found another one and licked that all over, too. Eventually she got up, and the pups all fell over on the newspaper. There they stayed, crawling over each other.

The clock in the living room struck seven, and Di went into Mike's room.

He was lying face down with his head in his hands. Di tiptoed over to his bed and leaned over him. She saw his body slowly moving up and down as he breathed, so she crept into the bed beside him and pulled the quilt over both of them.

"Wake up, Mike," she whispered in his ear. "I've got something to show you." She tickled the back of his neck.

Mike turned and stared at her face. "'Lo, Di." They smiled at each other.

"Come and see Fendy's puppies," said Di, trying to make a puppy out of her hands. "Puppies —do you understand? Tiny little puppies." She clenched her fist into a little ball.

Mike looked at his fingers, then did as Di had done, spread them out and then clenched his fist. "Me, too." Then he spread them out again.

Di laughed, picked him up and carried him out into the hall over to the dog-basket.

"See," said Mike, pointing at the small, black

bodies lying close to their mother. "See!" He struggled, trying to get down.

Di held his hand and placed it over one of the puppies. "Be very careful," she said, running his hand up and down the little pup.

Mike let her do it.

"Pussy," he said, looking at Di.

"No, they're not pussies. They're puppies. Fendy's puppies."

Mike shook his head. "Pussy," he said. "Nice pussy."

"All right, then. They're pussies."

Di found the one with the piece of wool around its neck and lifted it up.

Mike wanted to lift one up, too. He grasped one and pulled it away from the others. The puppy whined and Mike almost dropped it.

"Put it down," said Di, hearing how cross her voice sounded. She didn't believe she could be really cross with Mike. "You might drop it, don't you understand?"

But Mike didn't understand anything. The puppy squealed and Mike squeezed.

"Give it to me!"

Di took the struggling bundle and put it carefully back in the basket. "Let's go back to bed." She took Mike's hand and pulled him with her into his room. "It's only seven o'clock and the pups are terribly tired. Shall I read to you for a while?"

She lifted him on to the bed and fetched his picture book. There were all kinds of animals in the book—horses and cows, pigs and kittens, birds and dogs.

Di read the names out to him and Mike pointed.

"Pussy," he said, his small finger pressed on the nose of a calf.

"No, that's a calf. Moooo!"

Mike looked at Di in terror.

"All calves say 'moooo'. Cows and calves say 'moo'," said Di, making her mouth into a circle and mooing again. "Now let's find a picture of a pussy and a puppy, and then you'll know the difference."

Di leafed through the book and found a large white cat and a little black kitten.

"Pussy," said Mike, smiling broadly and putting his hand on the kitten.

"That's right. That's a little puss. Miaow, miaow," said Di, and Mike imitated her.

"Miaow, miaow."

They went on through the book and found a puppy, pale brown with dark eyes.

"That's a little puppy. Just like Fendy's. 'Bow-wow', it says."

But Mike shook his head.

"Yes, it is. It's a puppy. That's not a pussy." Di barked again. "Bow-wow."

Mike shook his head even more.

Suddenly he whined like Fendy's puppy had

and then laughed so much that the quilt shook.

Di laughed, too.

"You're right. Puppies don't bark. They whine."

Martin

They all wanted to hear about the puppies at
school. Di told them, during the first break. She
told them about having to help with the first
puppy because Fendy had been too tired, and
about the three that had been born during the
night after she had gone to bed. They all listened,
Martin, too, standing just behind Helen, but he
didn't say anything.

Not then, but he did later on, in the last break.

"Hey, Lanky Longlegs, can I come back with
you to see the pups?"

Lanky Longlegs. He was calling her Lanky
Longlegs. Di felt her face going hot and red, but
she didn't bat an eyelid.

"I had a dog last year. But it died just before
Christmas." Martin looked down at the asphalt.
"It was a Rottweiler, just like yours." He seemed
to be trying to dig a hole in the asphalt. "He was
run over by a truck. He was only a pup, and
dashed under the wheel."

Di felt the warmth running out of her face and
down into her stomach, burning her.

Run over!

"May I?" said Martin.

"Yes," she answered slowly, "if you promise
not to keep calling me Lanky Longlegs."

"Don't you like it?"

"No."

"I promise."

They were supposed to write something in the last class, but Di could do nothing. She kept thinking about the puppy and the truck.

She shuddered and tried to get rid of her horrible thoughts, but they wouldn't go away.

Martin was leaning over his paper, writing quickly across the white page.

Di looked at his back and hand, feeling something good inside her. She picked up her pencil and started to write.

Fendy growled when Di came with all her friends. She sat up in the basket and glared at them.

"It's only me," said Di, bending down and patting her. "And these are my friends. They only want to look at your puppies."

Fendy lay down again. Di's friends stood in the doorway.

"Only one at a time." That was Martin's voice. "One at a time, or Fendy'll be frightened."

He pushed Helen towards the basket and took the others with him out to the kitchen.

"This one was born first," said Di, lifting up the one with the red wool around its neck.

The puppy whined loudly, its legs working. But then it curled up and lay quite still in her hand. Di put the soft body against her cheek.

"Isn't it sweet?" said Helen.

"Do you want to hold it?"

Di handed the puppy to her so Helen could feel its little heart beating under the thin skin.

They were all allowed to look at the puppies and hold one. They came in one by one, just as Martin had said, and Fendy was quite calm all the time.

Martin stayed after the others had gone and sat with the pups, while Di took Fendy out. The dog ran down the steps over to the fence, where she barked twice to tell everyone that she was out and about again, then she squatted down, did what she had come for, and ran back.

Martin put the puppies on the floor. They crawled in all directions, looking for Fendy. Their legs wobbled and gave way under them, so they slid on their stomachs, heads bumping on the floor.

Fendy stood amongst them, nudging the puppies towards the basket with her nose.

"Look at that one, trying to feed off its mother's leg," said Martin, laughing.

Di changed the newspapers, putting the wet ones in a pile by the kitchen door, and lifted the pups back in the basket. Martin helped her. Fendy stood watching, and when all the pups were back in, she got in with them and lay down.

"Can I come again?" said Martin, taking the dirty papers out to the kitchen.

"Maybe," said Di from behind him.

"Maybe my dad will buy a puppy from you."

"Maybe."

Di didn't want to think about selling any of the pups, although she knew they couldn't keep them all, but she just didn't want to think about it.

Not now, anyhow.

The Bet

Di was late for school the next day. The dog-basket had looked like a pigsty and she had had to clean it out before leaving.

She ran the last bit, her books bumping in her bag which banged against her body.

Martin caught up with her before she reached the school entrance.

"Lanky Longlegs!"

Di stopped. "You promised you wouldn't call me that."

"I forgot." Martin shrugged his shoulders. "But listen, I asked my dad if he would buy one of your pups, and he said *yes*."

"You can't have one," said Di, trying to get her breath back. She was cross. "One, you can't have a pup, and two, you'll have to start remembering things."

"Remembering what? Not to call you Lanky Longlegs?"

"Yes." Di looked straight at him.

"Why can't I have one?" said Martin, grabbing her shoulder. "Why not?"

Di was scared. He was hurting her shoulder. "We're not going to sell them." She wriggled, and Martin let go.

"Keep nine Rottweilers?" said Martin, loudly

32

laughing. "You'll have to move. The dogs will take up all the space."

"You can't have one, anyhow."

"Because I call you Lanky Longlegs?"

"Partly."

"What if I promise to call you Diana Christine Sophie Mathilda?"

"You'd just forget. You never keep your promises."

"What if I promise to call you Di, then?"

"Maybe."

"I promise."

"I've heard that before."

"I didn't know you could be so cross."

Martin dashed into school ahead of her.

Di was late and Martin already in his place when she went into the classroom. The teacher was in a bad mood. But that didn't matter. Di was in a bad mood herself. Martin grinned scornfully at her when she sat down.

They had English first lesson. Di got out her English book. Martin pulled out his slingshot, put a pencil-sharpener in the sling and aimed down the row at Helen. Her papers scattered as the sharpener landed amongst them. She jumped and turned around.

Martin pretended not to notice and sat playing with his slingshot under the desk. Then he put a stump of pencil into the sling and aimed again.

The pencil went whizzing through the air and hit Helen on the back of the neck.

"Stop it!" she cried, scarlet in the face.

"I only wanted my sharpener back," said Martin, holding out his hand. Helen shook her head as she tossed it to him.

Di was miserable. She stared down at the lid of her desk, thinking about Martin.

But not as she had done yesterday. Then she had been thinking about his puppy, and how much she really liked him. Now, she didn't like him. He made her say such silly things. . .

During the last class the teacher went to the staff-room. Martin was cleaning the blackboard. This was his job for the week and he spent ages over it, and a great deal of water. Water splashed all over the floor.

"Shall I give her cushion a dose, too?" he called out, holding the sponge over the blue, foam rubber cushion on the chair behind the teacher's desk.

"You daren't," said Helen, putting down her pencil.

"What do you bet?"

Martin squeezed the sponge in his hand and water streamed down on to the cushion.

"Bet you an ice-cream cone you daren't say you did it!"

"All right."

More water. Martin went like a yo-yo between the bucket of water and the cushion.

34

"That'll do." He poked his finger into the cushion and put the sponge away.

They were sitting bolt upright when the teacher came back. There was a deathly silence in the room when she sat down.

They were having geography, and she swung around in her chair and pulled down the map of the world.

"Jerusalem," she said, pointing her stick somewhere east of the Mediterranean. "Jerusalem is in Israel." She drew a little circle with the pointer. "Originally it was . . ."

The pointer banged on the desk and she jumped up holding her behind and stared down at the chair.

"I'm . . ." She got no further. "Who did this?"

She stood there looking down the rows of desks, her gaze stopping at Ben, whose face was scarlet. But it often was. Di held her breath and saw that Martin was doing the same.

"I did."

Di felt Martin's desk being pushed forward as he got to his feet.

"I did it."

Martin remained standing.

He was made to stay in.

Helen and Di were behind the bicycle shed when their teacher disappeared out of the school gate.

"I'll go and buy that ice-cream cone." Helen

ran to a local shop and came back with a large one.

"I bought a chocolate one. Are you coming with me?"

But Di preferred to wait outside.

Helen was away for more than half an hour, and Di was cross at having to wait.

"What a long time you were!"

"We were talking. He's quite nice."

"I don't think so," said Di, kicking a stone and starting off towards home.

"He's awfully brave. Did you see how angry she was?" said Helen. "I'd never have dared do that. Say I'd done it, I mean."

Helen took the stone away from Di and threw it right across the road. It hit the edge of the pavement on the other side.

"Neither would I."

"But it was funny. Anyhow, when she sat down. Did you see her clutching her behind?" Helen started to laugh.

"I didn't think it all that funny," said Di, who was not laughing.

"It was only water. That's not too bad. I know some who've done much worse things."

"I don't think he ought to have done it, anyhow."

"Go on. She'll be dry by now, and she'll have forgotten all about it tomorrow."

They went on in silence.

The Adder

The wind smelled of autumn. It stung their cheeks and rocked the trees, sending leaves swirling through the air and down to the ground.

Di was packing her bag with her raincoat and rubber boots, woolly sweater and jeans.

"Don't forget your toothbrush," Mum called from the living room. "And a spare pair of thick socks."

"No, I won't." Mike was helping Di pack.

This was not the first time Di had been away from home. Last year she had spent a weekend with Helen in the mountains and met Martha who lived on a small farm nearby with her goats.

"See," said Mike, pointing at the nightgown lying on Di's sweater. "See."

"That's my nightgown. I'm sleeping at Helen's. At their cabin in the mountains. But I'll be back soon."

"Di go?" Mike frowned.

"Yes, but Di's coming back soon." Di felt a jab inside her. She remembered the evening Dad had told her about Mike's illness and how pale he had been when they had taken him to the hospital.

"You must look after the puppies for me while I'm away," she said, squatting down and putting her arms around Mike. "And help Mum clean up after them and make things easy for Fendy.''

She patted his cheek and gave him her tooth-brush to put in the bag.

Mike pressed it down with both hands and the toothbrush disappeared into the nightgown.

Dad and Mum and Mike stood in the window waving as Di went off with Helen and her parents. Mike waved the most, waving with his whole body, and Di waved back.

It was almost dark by the time they had reached the cabin. The wind had died down and the sun had gone, though it was still shining behind the mountains. A short distance away Di could see Martha's cabin.

Next morning the wind was blowing up on the mountain again, shaking the dwarf birches. They lay flat against the heather and let the wind blow over them.

The sun climbed over the mountain to find Helen and Di still asleep. They were tired after the car ride the day before and slept late.

After breakfast they put on their rubber boots and went out. The mountain rose high in front of them.

Helen wanted to climb to the top.

''Are we allowed to?'' asked Di, who thought it looked risky.

''Yes, as long as we stay on this side so that Mum and Dad can see us. It's not very far.''

They took sandwiches and oranges with them. And their jackets. Everything was put in Di's bag.

Helen went first because she knew the way, following a pathway to the foot of the mountain. There it divided into three. Helen chose the middle path.

Here and there they could see tracks made by Martha's goats, but apart from the tracks and some droppings, only the downtrodden heather told them they were on a path.

It was heavy going, the path uneven and bumpy. Their boots sank into the ground, which was soft and damp from the frost that had melted in the morning sun.

They climbed up the steeply winding path.

Halfway up they could see the bare peak.

"Let's stop for a while," said Helen, climbing on to a large boulder. Di followed.

"We can see the end of the world now," said Helen. "If the world wasn't round, we could see Africa." She pointed at the sun, which looked like a marble in the sky. "If there'd been any clouds today, we could have looked down on them." Helen swung an arm round in a great arc. "Sometimes the clouds make a white ring around the mountain, and you can see nothing but the peak growing out of them. I wonder if the clouds look the same on both sides?"

"They're either white or black," said Di, starting to peel her orange.

"I wonder if the lightning's above the clouds?" said Helen.

"I think it's inside them," said Di. "Dad told me that when two clouds collide, they explode and the lightning flashes."

They shared the orange between them.

"Just imagine sitting up here and looking down on lightning, Di," said Helen. "Watching it explode below, without being scared. Lightning never strikes upwards."

Helen spat out a pip, sending it soaring in a wide arc before it disappeared.

"Do you like Martin?" asked Di, pulling some moss off the stone they were sitting on.

"Yes. Don't you?"

"I don't know. He's so silly," said Di, crumbling the moss in her fingers.

"You mean he calls you Lanky Longlegs?"

"Well, there's that. And he shouts it out all over school, too."

Di looked down at her legs. "Do you think I've got skinny legs?"

"I think you've got Martin on the brain."

"Silly. Do you think I'm as tall as my name is long?"

"Taller."

Helen started laughing and gradually Di did, too, and they laughed until their voices rang all over the mountain.

"Take no notice of him," said Helen at last.

''No one else does. He'll stop one day.'' She got up and brushed moss off her jeans. ''Come on, we must get to the top.''

The wind was waiting for them up there, blowing between the rocks and snatching at their jackets.

''We're there!'' said Helen, flinging out her arms. ''Can you see Africa?''

''No, but I can see China.''

''Isn't it marvellous being able to see so far,'' cried Helen. ''It's too windy, though. Let's go down again.''

They pulled their hoods up and started down.

It was more difficult going down than up. Helen slipped on a loose stone, lost her balance and slid down until she came to a dwarf birch and could grab at its branches.

''Ow!''

Di leaped, slid and ran down at her cry. Helen had cut her hand on a sharp stone and blood was dripping from it.

Di got out her handkerchief and tied it around Helen's hand.

They were more careful on the last bit down to the big boulder.

They stopped there to rest for a moment. Helen looked at her bandage, and Di threw stones, throwing them straight out into the air and watching them vanish beneath her.

She missed with one stone and, instead of soaring away, it fell just behind her.

There was a sudden hiss behind them...

Turning, they saw a snake curled up like a garden hose. It was almost black with a zig-zag pattern down its spine.

The adder raised its head and flicked out its tongue, stretching and then drawing back its flat head. Suddenly it thrust its head forward again, only a few yards from them.

Di felt herself stiffen.

"We must get away," said Helen, not moving —forcing the words out of her mouth. She started sliding backwards.

Di stared at the snake. She saw the long body free itself and wriggle on to the stone, until it was lying on the edge, its head swaying.

Her whole body was aching, her throat dry, and she found it hard to swallow.

The adder jerked again when Helen disappeared behind the stone. Di held her breath and waited for it to attack her.

"Hurry!" cried Helen, but Di could not move. She sat quite still, staring hypnotized at the snake, her heart thumping and her hands clammy.

After what seemed like eternity, the snake curled up again and stayed there, its tongue flicking in and out. Then, silently, it slid off the stone and disappeared.

Di waited for a moment and then jumped down to where Helen crouched.

Martha

The wind howled around the cabin walls next morning.

Di opened the window and a cold blast rushed into the room.

"Oh, what weather!" She closed the window to shut it all out. "Will that adder freeze to death?"

"No, it'll go under the heather and hide," said Helen, who was sitting on the top bunk, dangling her legs.

The room was square and small, a wood-stove in one corner and a table with a basin and mug on it in the other. Both the white, china mug and basin were covered with brown cracks, the cracks like scratches that had grown together. Di was frightened every time she had to take the mug and basin out to the kitchen for water, afraid they would fall to pieces.

There was a wood-stove in the kitchen too, an old-fashioned black one. Instead of solid plates on top, it had a set of rings that reminded her of the coiled adder.

Helen's father used an iron hook to lift away the rings before filling the stove with wood shavings. When he lit the fire the flames sometimes burst out of the stove. Then he took the rings and put them back over the flames so that the fire was shut inside.

The cabin smelt of wood-stove and paraffin—a sweet, heavy kind of smell that covered everything —the window-sills, chairs, table and walls. Even the beds.

There was a long wooden table in the living room that was several hundred years old, almost white with age, and covered with scratches.

Di had asked Helen's mother what the children who had scratched the table had been like, but she had said she didn't think children had done it. Then Di had asked what kind of grown-ups would have used the breadknife cutting straight on to the table.

The wind died down later on and the dark clouds retreated northwards, leaving only the mountain mist.

Helen and Di looked out of the window, only just able to see across to Martha's small farm and her cabin, lying there like a dark shadow in the mist. Martha was inside the shadow, washing milking-pails and clearing out goat manure. There was a strong smell at Martha's, and Martha and her clothes smelled.

Martha was alone now that her husband Jonas was dead, but she had always run the summer pasture and the goats. They had had no children, but a great many pigs and goats.

Martha kept only goats now. Jonas's nephew ran the farm in the valley, but not the summer pasture. That was Martha's.

Jonas had died the year before. He had had chest trouble and attacks rather like whooping-cough. The doctor gave him pills, but they hadn't helped and, just before Martha was due to go up the mountain for the summer, he had died.

Now Jonas was buried in the churchyard, and Martha had planted flowers on his grave—red roses and forget-me-nots.

Di looked over at the cabin, remembering the day last year when Martha had talked about Jonas.

"Where's Jonas now?" she had asked. "Is he just in the ground?" Helen and Di had been sitting on the kitchen bench, eating waffles.

"Yes, Jonas is in the earth," Martha had said as she washed the milking-pails. "And as the years go by he will become more and more of the earth. Just like the leaves in the autumn. If they lie there long enough, they become soil."

Martha had put the milking-pails away and taken out the coffee pot.

"Don't you think Jonas is with God?"

"No, I don't believe in God and angels. Jonas is in the ground. He liked working the soil. He liked growing things, seeing them getting bigger and bigger. It says in the Bible that it is from the soil we've come, and to the soil we'll go, and I believe that."

"It's a pity you don't think Jonas is with God."

"Why?"

"Because everything's good about God. That's what my teacher says."

"Jonas is all right, even if he isn't with God. He doesn't have to cough and try to get his breath any longer. That was terrible for him."

Martha had crunched a sugar-lump.

"But you know, I often talk to him," she had said. "I talk about all the things I learned from him and about everything we did together. I talk to him when I put flowers on his grave, and then it's almost as if he was with me again."

"Do you think he was glad to die?" Di had asked, taking a sugar-lump.

"I don't think he knew he was going to die. But when he did, when he no longer had to struggle for his breath, he looked calm and happy. Handsome, he was, too—lying in his coffin."

Martha had washed down the rest of the sugar-lump with hot coffee.

But that was last year.

Di and Helen had talked about Jonas the night before, and about heaven and churchyards.

"My uncle's dead, too," Di had said. "He was drowned on his summer holidays. They never even found the boat. He's in heaven now, Mum says."

"Isn't he in the churchyard?"

"No, he's in heaven."

"I'd rather be in the churchyard, when I die," Helen had said as she blew out the paraffin lamp. "Then Mum can plant roses and forget-me-nots."

The Kid

Helen jumped down from her bunk and stared into the mist. A shadow was looming out of it. It was Martha, coming towards their cabin.

"Martha's coming," cried Helen. "Let's get dressed and go back with her."

They dressed quickly, but Martha was already in the living room when they went in.

"They're down in the gully and the kid's injured. Must be its leg," Martha was saying in a quiet voice, but they could tell she was worried.

"I'll come with you, Martha," said Helen's father.

"Well, if it isn't Helen," cried Martha, hugging her. "I was just asking your dad if he'd help me with a goat and a kid I can't get out of the gully." She patted Helen's cheek. "And Di's here, as well, I see. You'll be a help, too."

Helen's father was standing by the door, ready to go. "Come on, Martha. We mustn't waste any time."

"Can we come, too, Dad?" asked Helen. "Please!"

"Not in this mist. Supposing you got lost."

"We could be roped together," Helen persisted. "Tie the rope around our waists, like we've done before. It's not very far, and Di can walk just as fast as I can.''

Helen was quite out of breath from talking so quickly.

''Oh, all right then. Get the rope from the shed, and put some warmer clothes on.''

Di found herself in the middle, with the rope in a noose around her waist, Helen behind her, and the shadowy figures of Martha and Helen's father in front, all looped together by the rope.

The cabin vanished from sight into the mist which made the air thick and grey with moisture.

Drops ran down their cheeks like tears. They followed the sheep paths around the mountain, the night frost lying on it like a white blanket. The dwarf birches looked white and crooked in the mist.

Martha and Helen's father walked briskly. Although her back was bent, Martha climbed as nimbly as a goat up the path. Di followed, trying to find the same rhythm, but it was difficult. She kept slipping and missing her footing, and the rope kept jerking at her waist. Under her shirt she was sweating. She gasped for breath as she climbed on, her heart banging like a drum. Thinking about the nanny-goat refusing to leave her kid helped. Things must be much worse for the kid than for her. Supposing it had broken its leg like a snapped stick. Di felt another jerk on the rope.

At last Martha and Helen's father stopped. Di had no idea where they were, whether on the mountain top or behind it, or on some ridge or other.

They stood still listening. Not a sound. The mountain seemed to be sleeping. They couldn't even hear the mountain streams.

Martha cupped her hands and hullooed into the mist.

There was an echo, and the sound came bouncing back to them. Then they heard a bleat from below, and Martha called again. "It's down there," she said, pointing in front of her.

"I'll climb down and call if I need help," said Helen's father, untying the knot and giving the rope to Martha. Then he vanished into the mist.

A moment later, they heard him calling.

"Its left leg is injured, but I don't think it's broken." His voice came from inside the mist. Not long after, he appeared, hunched over, with the injured kid slung on his shoulder.

"I think it has injured its foot," he said, putting the animal down on the moss. The kid tried to get up, but couldn't, and the nanny-goat stood over it, comforting it with long, anxious bleats.

Helen opened her bag and took out two bowls and a plastic bottle of milk.

"You think of everything, Helen," said Martha, giving her a hug. She bent down with one of the bowls for the kid, which was lying with one leg straight out. It drank the milk greedily, the nanny-goat at its side, rubbing her head against Martha's leg. She wanted some milk, too, and Helen had to fill her bowl three times.

The trip down was easier. Di found a rhythmic way of walking that suited the uneven ground and pace.

The wind rose on the way back, blowing away the mist. The sun came through and the autumn heather and moss shone yellow, red and white.

Martha examined the kid when they got back to her cabin. She bandaged the bad foot firmly and made a comfortable place for the kid just inside the door.

"I think you're right," she said to Helen's father. "It's not broken. A few days' rest will probably do the trick." She bent down and tickled the kid under its jaw. "Thanks for your help."

They all went into Martha's kitchen and she gave them waffles and real goat's cheese, her own home-made goat cheese. There was nothing like it. She also gave them a whole pile of waffles to take back with them. Di planned to give some to Mike.

The Photographs

Di had hoped Mike would be awake when she arrived home from the mountains, and she ran straight into his room. But he was fast asleep, lying on his stomach, his thumb in his mouth. She put the waffles down beside his bed and closed the door behind her.

Things changed in various ways, both good and bad, after her trip to the mountains. Di noticed it at school in the very first lesson.

It was something to do with Martin, who would not look at her or speak to her.

At least he had stopped calling her Lanky Longlegs, but it was silly of him not to call her anything at all.

Martin was odd for several weeks. The puppies grew and Martin remained silent, spending all the breaks with Dan, whispering secrets that were for them alone.

Dad had taken some photographs of the pups and Di took them with her to school. She wanted Martin to see them, and she pushed them over on to his desk.

As she did so, she realized why he was behaving so oddly. It was the *puppy*.

Of course, it was the puppy—the puppy she'd

said he couldn't have. That was why ... But she hadn't really meant it.

Di carefully took the photographs back. Martin pretended not to notice.

Afterwards she sat looking at his back and bent head, which seemed to be saying to her that she was stupid and kept forgetting things, forgetting that he had once had a puppy.

She certainly hadn't forgotten. On the contrary, she kept remembering. But at least she knew now why he wouldn't speak to her.

Di talked to Helen about it in break.

"I know why Martin won't talk to me," she said. "It's because I said he couldn't have one of the puppies."

"Why not?"

"I just said it."

"Why?"

"Because he kept calling me Lanky Longlegs."

"He was only teasing!"

"Yes, that's why."

"But that's silly."

"Yes," agreed Di.

"I know what you should do, Di," said Helen. "Forget all that business about your name. When I was small and my braids stuck out straight and I had freckles, they used to call me Pippi Longstocking, and that was just as bad."

"Hm."

"Tell Martin he can have the puppy, and that

you didn't really mean what you said."

"I don't want to. And he wouldn't listen, anyhow."

"Write him a note, then, and put it on his desk."

Di didn't have to write a note because he spoke to her the very next day while their teacher was out of the room.

"Hey, Di. You *are* going to sell those pups, aren't you?" he asked as he sharpened a pencil.

Di felt her heart thumping again.

"Dan said he'd been to your house yesterday with his father," Martin went on.

Di pretended to be looking in her bag.

"He said he'd bought one of the dogs."

Di found a book and started leafing through it.

"Is Dan the only one who's going to be allowed to buy one?" persisted Martin.

"I didn't mean it," said Di, shutting her book. "I didn't mean what I said." She could feel herself going red.

"Why did you say it, then?"

"Because you were hurting my shoulder."

"Is that why I couldn't have one?"

"And you got so angry."

"Didn't you see that was because you were so cross with me?" said Martin.

"No, not until later. Only you didn't want to look at the photographs of the pups."

Di looked down at the lid of her desk.

The teacher came back and closed the door behind her.

"Open your French books on page fifty-six."

There was a lot of rustling and shuffling, and Di leaned forward.

"You *can* have one if you want to," she said. She bent down over her bag again. "I'll ask Dad," she went on.

Martin leaned back and whispered to Di: "I've something to show you at home. I'll bring it with me to school tomorrow."

What he wanted to show her was a red collar with a metal nameplate. He had wrapped it up in green tissue paper.

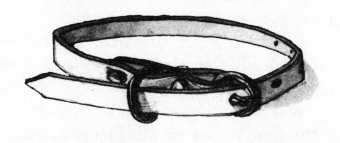

"I was given it for Christmas last year. It was meant for my puppy." Martin put it down on the desk. "I never used it, but I can now, can't I?" He fingered the red collar. "Do you want to hold it?"

Di turned the collar over in her fingers – it was the grandest collar Di had ever seen, soft and good to feel, with a shiny nameplate. Fendy had a brown one, like most dogs, and hers was much bigger. This one was quite small and bright red, a proper puppy-collar.

"I've a lead, too."

Martin pulled something red out of his satchel.

He clipped the lead to the collar and pulled it across the desk.

"Bow-wow," he barked. Di smiled, and the teacher told them to be quiet.

Di lay awake for a long time that night, thinking about the woollen thread, the red collar, and the puppy. If it ever became hers, then it, too, would have a red collar with a metal nameplate.

She fell asleep and dreamed about small, black puppies and red collars.

Mike Is Ill

Late autumn came and the leaves fell off the trees. The sun shone but there was no warmth in it.

The puppies grew bigger and bigger week by week. By now they were like small bears with large heads and even larger paws. Di kept having to find longer pieces of red wool to tie around the neck of her special pup.

The puppies tormented Fendy, jumping up and nipping her coat. She would growl then and walk away from them. But she liked playing with them, shaking each by the scruff of the neck, turning them over on the floor and baring her teeth. Then the pups growled back at her.

Di and Mike made the food for the pups, mixing meat with milk and cod-liver oil. Di would add the eggs while Mike stirred with a spoon. They used the large frying pan. It was just big enough for all the puppies.

The first time the puppies had been given proper food, Mum had dealt out eight small portions on eight small plates. But she should never have done that.

The puppies simply didn't understand. They pushed the food over the edges and climbed on to the plates. They even piddled on the plates, making a terrible mess. That was when Mum thought of the old frying pan, and although some of them did still climb inside with the food now and again, there was much less mess than there was when using the plates.

The pups could smell the food, and whined with hunger. Fendy was out in the garden. She had had her meal and was scratching at the door, so Di let her in.

There were messy newspapers everywhere. Di collected them all and wiped the floor. "Mike, will it be ready soon?" she called. "The pups are terribly hungry." She heard Mike throwing down the spoon, and at that moment Fendy was sick all over the floor, her head down, the mess pouring out. Di gasped – Fendy didn't usually do that.

She could feel her gorge rising and coughed to get rid of the sick feeling.

"Mum, Fendy's been sick and the pups are eating it!" she shouted.

At that moment Mike arrived with the frying-pan full of food and very heavy, the mixture slopping back and forth as he walked. Mum came flying in, took the frying pan from Mike and laughed when she saw Di's terrified face.

"Is Fendy ill?" asked Di anxiously.

"No, no, she just realizes the pups are hungry, so she's giving them the food she's already chewed up."

Mum put the frying-pan down. "Fendy can have it instead," she said.

"Do dogs usually do that?" asked Di. "Being sick for their pups?"

"Not usually, but when dogs lived in the wild, they used to chew up the food for their pups to make it easier for them." Mum patted Fendy's head and spoke to her.

The floor was sticky where the mess had been, so Di fetched a bucket and cloth. The puppies bit at the cloth, fastening their sharp teeth into it and pulling.

"Stop it," said Di, pushing them away so that they slid across the floor, landing in the corner.

Mike was ill that night. The doctor came and said he must go to the hospital. Mum packed a small suitcase with the things Mike liked best—his teddy bear and his comforter-cloth, a little bit of an old quilt cover. He liked rubbing the piece of cloth against his cheek as he sucked his thumb.

Mike was asleep when Mum carried him out to the car. Di held his hand and pressed it—it was so small and warm. His hand was pale, though, like his face.

Mum said nothing, just nodded when Dad said they had to hurry.

The doctor, Mum and Dad all left together with Mike. Sister Anna came to be with Di, and Dad promised he would be back as soon as he could.

Sister Anna and Di made egg-toddies and Di was allowed to put in as much sugar as she liked.

"Have you seen a lot of children die?" asked Di, dipping her finger in and tasting it.

"Yes, a few."

"Does it hurt to die?" Di went on, licking her finger.

"No, it's like falling asleep, just like you do every night."

"Do people dream when they're dead?"

"No, not the way you dream. They don't do anything. They don't breathe or dream."

Sister Anna fetched some glasses.

"Do you know Mike has a very serious blood disease?" asked Di.

"Yes," said Sister Anna, pouring the toddies into the glasses. "Yes, I know. And I know what you're thinking. But we must think about Mike being with the doctors now—and they're doing everything they can for him."

She went into the living room.

Dad came home before Di had fallen asleep and sat down on the edge of her bed, holding her hand.

"You'll have to be a big girl now and help me with things here at home while Mike's in the hospital."

"Yes, but what about Mum? Is she going to stay there, too?"

"No, not all the time, but she can stay there

whenever she wants to. They've given her a bed just beside Mike's.''

"Can I go and see him?"

"I don't think so. The doctors are terribly strict about children visiting. I think they're afraid of infection.''

"Could I catch it then?"

"No, no, it's not that. I think the doctors are afraid visitors will bring infections with them into the hospital.''

"Oh. Did Mike cry?" said Di, remembering the feel of his small hand in hers.

"No, he just smiled a little, and then fell asleep again. But you must go to sleep now, too, and I'll get your breakfast tomorrow morning. You can have two eggs, if you like.''

"Just one, please.''

Di pulled the quilt up to her chin and turned her head to the wall.

Dad went out, closing the door behind him.

Di lay there listening to the sounds outside. Dad was tidying up in the kitchen and she could hear the water running and glasses tinkling.

Dad always made a noise clearing up in the kitchen. Mum often said he made more noise— and mess—than Di did.

Di usually liked hearing Dad making a noise, but she didn't this evening. She didn't like anything this evening. Everything was wrong—miserable and wrong—and there was no one to share it with.

Not even Dad. He wanted to be miserable alone. Di had realized that his thoughts were elsewhere, somewhere she wasn't allowed.

If only Mum were home. Di felt the lump inside her growing, and she pressed her nose into the quilt.

The Stars

The next day, Martin and his father came to look at the puppies. They wanted a female.

"They don't roam as much," Martin's father said, lifting up the one with the red wool thread round its's neck. "I think we'll have this one." He shook the puppy gently by the scruff of its neck.

Di couldn't believe her ears. She stared down at the floor, her eyes smarting.

"No, that's Fendy's first-born, so we'd like to keep that one a little longer," her father said. Although his voice was gentle, Di could hear that he was quite definite.

They chose one of the other bitches instead and Martin put the collar over the pup's head. The puppy yelped and rolled on the floor, trying to get the collar off with its forepaws. It succeeded, too! Di laughed.

"You'll have to wait until it's a bit bigger and —you'll see—it'll take to your collar," she said. Martin put the collar into his pocket and carried the pup away under his arm.

Mum stopped working at the travel agent's when Mike came back from the hospital.

Mike was almost the same, but only almost. He was just as good-natured, smiling as before, but his eyes weren't so bright, and he was nearly always tired. It didn't make any difference if Di played the games he liked most of all, he suddenly didn't want to any longer. He just went off to Mum who gave him some medicine, medicine from a bottle that he seemed to like less and less.

Mike was asleep when Di came home from school. She hoped he would be awake, but she was disappointed.

The door into his room was open and she could see him lying on his stomach with his thumb in his mouth.

She closed the door carefully and went out to the kitchen to her mother. She was terribly hungry because she'd forgotten her packed lunch and although Helen had shared hers, it hadn't been much.

She got out the bread and started slicing it.

"Mum, are things bad for Mike? He gets tired so quickly, now."

"No, it's just that he can't manage very much."

"Do you think he'll get well again?"

"I don't know, Di. We just have to hope."

Mum was staring ahead of her, her eyes dull. A broad sunbeam lay across the kitchen table, dividing the top into two, one light part, the other dark.

"Do you believe in God, Mum?"

"Yes, you know that."

"How can you believe in something you can't see?"

Mum went across to the window.

"Come over here, Di," she said. "Can you see the stars?"

"There aren't any stars in the sky in the daytime, are there?"

"Yes," said Mum. "There are stars in the sky day and night, but we just can't see them. The sun hides them, or rather shines more brightly than they do."

"Oh," said Di, staring up at the sky. It looked blue and empty, though it wasn't empty, but full of stars she couldn't see.

"Mum, why do only some people go to heaven?"

Di cut her bread in two.

"What do you mean?" asked her mother.

"Uncle John's in heaven, and Jonas is in the churchyard."

Mother went across to Di, lifted her up on to the bench and held her hand. "I don't think only some people go to heaven. I think everybody goes to heaven."

"Does everybody believe that?"

"No, not everyone."

"How do they get to heaven?"

"I don't know, Di dear. I don't even know what heaven is. All I know is that I believe in the soul, what's inside you." Mum put her hand on Di's chest. "The thing that feels good when things are good, and bad when something's bad, everything you think, everything you feel and everything you are, what's just you and not like any other person in the world—that doesn't die—even if your body does." Mum stopped for a moment. "So I believe there is a heaven."

She lifted Di down again and hugged her.

"Will Mike go to heaven when he dies?"

The words hung in the air between them. Then Mum's face crumpled, and tears ran down her face.

"Yes, Di, Mike will go to heaven when he dies."

Helen

It was Friday and winter had almost come. Helen was standing in a cloud of steam and smoke. The kitchen window was open and Di saw her waving her arms about, trying to get the smoke out through the window.

Helen had spilled waffle mixture on to the stove and the burnt lumps were sending up clouds of smoke.

"Hi, Di! How nice to see you and Fendy— and what a good thing you've come! I need your help."

Helen moved the waffle-iron and scraped off the black lumps with a knife. Even more smoke appeared. Helen coughed and wiped the knife on her apron.

"Did you make the mixture yourself?"

Di put a finger into it. The mixture was thick and smooth and tasted sweet.

"Yes, Mum told me how to. Three eggs, milk, sugar, flour and a little baking powder, and butter, of course. I was going to surprise Mum and Dad when they came home, but if I don't stop making such a mess, it will be rather more than a surprise!"

Helen laughed and put a damp cloth on the stove. "It keeps getting worse and worse!" A cloud of white steam rose from the cloth. Helen snatched it off and threw it into the sink.

"Open the window. The other one, too," cried Helen, and Di unfastened them and threw them open. Gradually the air cleared. After that, Helen was more careful about how much mixture she poured on to the waffle-iron.

"How quiet it is here," said Di. "Much quieter than it is at home." She looked around. "Mike and the puppies make an awful lot of noise. When Mike's awake, that is."

"There's only me here," said Helen. "It's nice, actually."

She poured on some more mixture. "No one bosses me about, and there's no one to fight with. Have you ever been to Mia's place? Oh, the noise! Six children and two dogs, and their mother's always shouting."

Helen shifted the waffle-iron.

"Do you know, when Mia's mum goes and buys new clothes for her, new shirts or a skirt or something, she always takes her younger sister with her. She decides, too, because the clothes will be *passed down* to her. Imagine that!"

Helen shook her head. "Imagine having a little sister who decided what your new clothes were to be!"

"Can I have one?" asked Di, as Helen put another pale brown waffle on the pile on the dish. "And can Fendy have one, too?"

Helen nodded, and Di bent down to Fendy, who was sniffing and pricking up her ears. She held out a paw and the waffle vanished down her throat.

"They're as good as Martha's," said Di, taking another one. "A little sweeter."

"Martha always makes cream waffles, but I couldn't find any cream, or I would've done, too. Do you want to take one home for Mike?"

Helen hunted for a plastic bag and found one in the drawer of the pan cupboard. "Is Mike going into the same hospital again?"

"I don't know, but I think so."

Di suddenly felt miserable. Mike had changed so much. He didn't laugh any longer—not in the way he used to—almost falling off the chair with laughter. He was mostly very quiet. And sad. Nothing was fun any more, and mostly he just wanted to be with Mum.

Di took a deep breath.

"It's awful Mike being ill," she said, taking a bite out of the waffle. "Mum keeps crying. I can hear her when I've gone to bed. And Dad comforts her. They talk about Mike dying then. But they don't talk about it to me. Only to each other. That's almost the worst."

Fendy pawed at her leg, hoping for some more waffle.

"Sometimes I want to go into their room when Mum cries, but the door's closed, so I don't.'' Di swallowed, feeling a jab of pain inside her.

"Is Mike going to die, then?" asked Helen.

"Mum thinks so."

"Has she said so?"

"No, but she said he'll go to heaven when he dies and, when she said that, she started crying."

Di felt the tears running down her cheeks, and she caught them with her tongue.

Helen at once put her arms around Di's neck and hugged her as if trying to hug away all the misery—or at least to share it with her.

Then she let go and went over to the waffle-iron and broke a waffle up into small, heart-shaped pieces.

Di rubbed her face and wiped her nose on the sleeve of her sweater.

"These are for Mike," said Helen, giving her the bag. "You can have some more if you like."

"I think that'll be enough," said Di, taking the bag and smiling. "Helen, no one knows. About Mike. You won't say anything to anyone, will you?"

"Promise I won't," said Helen, putting out her hand. "Promise on my honour."

They stood looking at each other.

Then the clock in the living room struck five and Di pulled her hand out of Helen's with a start. "I must run. I promised to be home by five o'clock."

Helen went with her to the door and let her and Fendy out. Fendy ran, barking, down the steps.

"Are you going to keep that last puppy?"

"I don't know. It is the only puppy left. We've sold the others. Dad hasn't said anything definite, but he knows I hope we can keep it," said Di, watching Fendy. "I must hurry—supper's at six, and I'm five minutes late already."

She gave Helen a quick hug and hurried down the steps.

Mike Dies

Winter came on the third day of December, the clouds low over the roofs and frost on the window-panes, making patterns like shooting-stars. Di drew back the curtains and looked at the snow falling.

She didn't feel like getting up. She felt empty inside, as if she had lost something.

Mike was in the hospital again. Mum and Dad had taken him in the day before, and Dad had come back alone. Mum was to stay there.

They had played cards the evening before, Dad and Di. But it hadn't been much fun. They had pretended to be thinking about the game, but they were really thinking about something quite different. Dad had tried to smile and joke, and so had Di. But it had been impossible. She wanted to talk about Mike, but there was something that stopped her.

Di watched the snow melting on the window-pane, wondering when Mum would come back from the hospital. Perhaps she was going to stay there all day? But she would be sure to 'phone. Di sighed. How awful everything was. She would like to sleep all day. She drew the curtains and crept under her quilt again.

Di didn't know how long she'd slept, or whether she had slept at all. She only knew the telephone had woken her.

She jumped out of bed, wondering what the time was.

Dad answered the telephone and Di crept closer to him. She could hear Mum's voice. It was different, thick in an odd way, and tired.

"Yes," said Dad, bending forward, holding the telephone in one hand and resting his head on the other. Di couldn't hear what Mum was saying, but she saw Dad sink down on to the chair.

"We'll come at once." Dad covered his eyes with his hand, and Di saw the tears running down his cheeks and chin and on to his trousers.

Then she knew. Then she knew better than a thousand words could have told her, and something went stiff inside her—freezing into ice. Her eyelids were burning, but no tears came. There was only one thought in her mind. Mike.

Di didn't sleep that night. The day had been too awful, and she had felt she might fall to pieces, be torn to pieces, the misery in her bursting her open. She had hardly been able to cry, either. Only once. That was when they fetched Mum from the hospital and Mum had had Mike's teddy bear under her arm. Then Di had had to bite her lip to stop herself from screaming. She had run to

Mum and hidden her head in her coat, and only then had she noticed her tears.

Helen came the next afternoon. They skipped in the basement and Di got hot and sweaty. Tired, too. That was good in a way. It helped being able to feel something else, apart from all the hurt.

Helen stayed for supper, and Mum made oatmeal porridge with lots of sugar in it.

Helen never had oatmeal porridge at home and she never tried to make it herself, either. She just couldn't be bothered to. She only ever wanted to eat it at Di's.

Fendy and the puppy were given the rest of the porridge. The pup was housetrained now and whined at the kitchen door every time it wanted to go out. It had piddled on the floor inside only once. The puppy had grown large, too—strong around the neck and broad across the chest. Di had had to replace the wool collar yet again.

The pup was sitting beside her, holding out its paw.

"Go to bed. No more," said Di, slapping its back and shoving it towards the passage.

Dad sat on the edge of her bed for a long time that night, reading to her, and Di said her prayers to him, clasping her hands so hard, her knuckles turned white.

"Are things difficult for Mike now?" asked

Di, taking the teddy bear and hugging it.

"No, it's us it's difficult for now," said Dad, stroking her hair.

"Shall we plant flowers on his grave?"

Dad nodded.

"May I do that?"

"Yes, as many as you like."

"Then I'll plant roses and forget-me-nots."

The Dream

Di had a dream that night. She dreamed about moss and clouds. And Mike.

They were up in the mountains at Helen's, running across the heather and birch roots, rolling around in the moss and hugging each other. And Mike was laughing, just as he used to do.

The sky was low, the wind blowing great, black clouds above their heads.

The mountain was like a dark wall shutting off the world. They were alone. Just the two of them. Mike and Di. Happy to be together.

Suddenly one of the clouds seemed to burst apart and a broad sunbeam shone down on them. Heather and birches both changed, absorbing the light and throwing it back in yellow, red and gold.

The light was so sharp that Di had to screw up her eyes, but then it suddenly disappeared. The sunbeam vanished as quickly as it had come and the wind blew more clouds across, shutting out the sun.

Di turned to Mike, but she could not see him. He wasn't there any longer. She cried out, but her voice echoed back at her.

Then she cried again. And woke.

Di sat up in bed and clutched at the quilt, her whole body shivering.

She stared into the dark, her heart hammering, the echo of the cry still with her.

She felt the tears warm on her cheeks.

Carefully she slid out of bed and made her way to the door. The light was on, and Di slipped over to her parents' door. It was quiet in there and she could hear their even breathing.

She went into Mike's room.

It was dark and still. Di switched the light on and went over to his bed.

The pillow was there. And the quilt. But no Mike.

Then she heard the echo again—cutting through her—and she cried, her tears seeming to fill her whole body.

She threw herself down on to the bed.

Di woke to find Mum stroking her hair, bending over the bed. She looked as tired as that day when she had stood in the doorway and said she wished she could comfort away all the misery.

Di put her arms around her neck and pulled her down to her.

"I had a dream. I cried out, but you didn't hear me."

She sat up in bed. "I dreamed about Mike. We were up in the mountains at Helen's, playing. It was wonderful." Di tried to smile. "And Mike laughed just as he used to. Then something lovely happened.''

Mum squatted down and held on to her.

''At first it was cloudy, but suddenly one of the clouds parted and a sunbeam shone down on us. Then it disappeared. And Mike, too. I called out. And then I woke up.''

Di felt her mother holding on to her even harder.

"Do you think the sunbeam took him?"

Mum hugged Di and smiled, although there were tears in her eyes as she spoke.

"Yes, Di, dear, the sunbeam came and took him in your dream."

Then she lifted Di up and carried her to her own room.

The Collar

Di didn't feel like going to school. She thought everyone would be able to see what was going on inside her.

It was a dull day, the snow dirty, and nothing but wet pools under her boots.

"Hullo, Di!" Helen came running after her. "I've just been to your house, because I wanted to walk to school with you, but you'd already gone."

Helen took her hand.

"I met Martin on the corner, and I told him about Mike. I hope you don't mind. He was nice. He just stared at me without saying anything, then he ran back home again."

Helen dropped her hand and opened her bag.

"Look what Mum's made for us!"

She took out a bag of freshly baked buns. "There are raisins and orange peel in them."

Di thought Helen was the nicest girl in the world.

"We must hurry. The bell will ring in a minute."

Helen flung her bag on to her shoulder again and grabbed Di's hand.

Martin was late, but the teacher wasn't cross. She just said good morning to him and told him to sit down. That wasn't like her. But she wasn't her usual self at all. She started the day by reading *Robinson Crusoe* all through the first lesson. Usually she read only on Fridays, for the last lesson. But today was Monday, and first lesson, too.

She spoke to Di during the break. Mum had phoned to tell her about Mike, and she said Di didn't have to stay at school if she didn't want to. Helen could go home with her.

"I think I'll stay, especially if you're going to read more of that book," said Di, trying to look pleased.

And she was. A little. As long as she didn't think about Mike. Then everything froze to ice inside her, and she could feel nothing but a nasty, hard lump.

Martin didn't speak to her all day, nor did he look at her. He just sat there with his back half-turned to her.

But his back wasn't cross, just miserable. Di felt that. Martin was sorry and didn't know what to do, so he didn't look at her.

Di and Helen spent the breaks together.

They divided the buns into small pieces so that they had something to eat every break. They didn't say much. They had the buns and they had each other.

Helen and Di went home together after school. Helen had to go to the dentist, so she couldn't come in.

The sky was high and blue now and the sun low, drying up the puddles. All the snow had gone as if there had been no winter at all.

Di went into the living room where Mum was reading in the window. There were open envelopes on the table and a smell of flowers, a sweet, heavy smell that came from the mantelpiece. Mum's eyes were swollen and Di could see she had been crying.

She squatted down beside her and took her hand. Mum squeezed her hand. The pup came running in and slid on its backside along the floor when it tried to stop.

Mum got up and stroked Di's cheek, then went out into the kitchen.

"Martin brought this for you earlier today," she said, handing Di a flat red parcel.

"Oh, a present for me. How nice!" said Di, turning it over.

"Aren't you going to open it?"

"I was just trying to guess what it was."

"A book, perhaps?"

"But why should he give me a book?"

Di carefully untied the ribbon—white silk ribbon. That wasn't like Martin, but none of this was like Martin.

There was a cardboard box inside the red paper.

"No wonder he was late for school this morning, if he had to do all this," said Di, laughing. "Luckily teacher wasn't cross."

Di knew what it was as soon as she opened the box although there was green tissue paper inside.

It was round and thick to hold. It was long, too. But that was the lead. Di stood there with the collar in her hand. She couldn't make a sound.

The nameplate shone, and Di rubbed her finger up and down it.

She suddenly felt warm inside, a wave of delight rushing through her.

She stood there for a moment, and then she went over to the puppy to put on the collar.

The pup lay still as if it knew it had to, and Di bent down and broke the piece of red wool.

She hid her face in the soft, black fur, and cried.

Then she fastened the lead to the collar and pulled the puppy out of the basket. "Come on. Let's go for a walk."

The puppy shook its head and tried to bite the lead, but Di jerked it and the pup stopped.

They went out into the garden and Di sat down on the stone steps. She took the puppy into her arms and pressed it to her.

The evening came and took the day away, leaving only a little strip of light on the horizon which grew narrower and narrower, then vanished altogether.